/

BEATRIX POTTER'S
NURSERY RHYME BOOK

With new reproductions from the original illustrations

F. WARNE & Co.

FREDERICK WARNE
Penguin Books Ltd, Harmondsworth, Middlesex, England
Viking Penguin Inc., 40 West 23rd Street, New York, New York 10010, U.S.A.
Penguin Books Australia Ltd, Ringwood, Victoria, Australia
Penguin Books Canada Limited, 2801 John Street, Markham, Ontario, Canada L3R 1B4
Penguin Books (N.Z.) Ltd, 182–190 Wairau Road, Auckland 10, New Zealand

First published 1984
Reprinted 1984, 1985 (twice), 1986
This edition with new reproductions first published 1987
This arrangement of Beatrix Potter's works copyright © Frederick Warne & Co., 1984

ISBN 0 7232 3254 7

Printed in Great Britain by
William Clowes Limited, Beccles and London

Contents

Bow, wow, wow, whose dog art thou?

Bow, wow, wow!
    Whose dog art thou?
'I'm little Tom Tinker's dog,
    Bow, wow, wow!'

Knitting

Knitting, knitting, 8, 9, 10,
I knit socks for gentlemen;
I love muffin and I love tea;
Knitting, knitting, 1, 2, 3!

The mouse's find

I found a tiny pair of gloves
    When Lucie'd been to tea,
They were the dearest little loves—
    I thought they'd do for me—

I tried them—(quite inside them!)
    They were *much* too big for me!
I wear gloves with *one* button-hole
    When *I* go out to tea.

I'll put them in an envelope
    With sealing wax above,
I'll send them back to Lucie—
    I'll send them with my love.

Goosey Goosey Gander

Goosey, goosey, gander,
    Whither will you wander?
Upstairs and downstairs
    And in my lady's chamber!

There I met an old man
    That would not say his prayers,
So I took him by the left leg
    And threw him down the stairs!

If acorn-cups were tea-cups

If acorn-cups were tea-cups,
    what should we have to drink?
Why! honey-dew for sugar,
    in a cuckoo-pint of milk;
With pats of witches' butter
    and a tansey cake, I think,
Laid out upon a toad-stool
    on a cloth of cob-web silk!

Ride a cock-horse

Ride a cock-horse to Banbury Cross
To see a fine lady upon a white horse;
Rings on her fingers and bells on her toes,
And she shall have music wherever she goes!

I saw a ship a-sailing

I saw a ship a-sailing
A-sailing on the sea;
And Oh! it was all laden
With pretty things for thee!

There were comfits in the cabin
And apples in the hold;
The sails were made of silk
And the masts were made of gold.

And four and twenty sailors
That stood upon the decks
Were four and twenty white mice
With chains about their necks.

The captain was a guinea-pig—
The pilot was a rat—
And the passengers were rabbits
Who ran about, pit pat!

The old woman who lived in a shoe

You know the old woman who lived in a shoe,
And had so many children she didn't know what to do?
She gave them some broth without any bread,
She whipped them all round and put them to bed.
I'm sure if she lived in a little shoe house,
That little old woman was surely a mouse!

The see-saw

Two little mice were playing a game—
—Thingummy-jig and Whatzisname—
'You're too little and I'm too big,'
Said Whatzisname to Thingummy-jig.

'You're too tiny but *I* am too tall!'
'*I*'m enormous but *you* are too small!'
Up and down—'Why we're just the same!'
Said Thingummy-jig to Whatzisname.

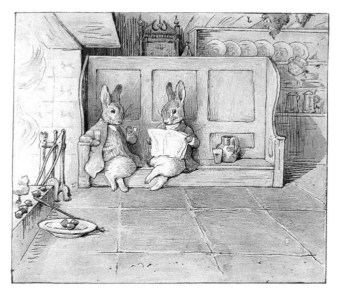

Cecily Parsley

Cecily Parsley lived in a pen,
And brewed good ale for gentlemen;

Gentlemen came every day,
Till Cecily Parsley ran away.

Old Mother Hubbard

Old Mother Hubbard
Went to the cupboard,
To get her poor dog a bone;
But when she got there
The cupboard was bare,
And so the poor doggie had none.

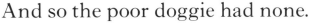

She went to the baker's
To buy him some bread,
But when she came back
The poor dog was dead.

She went to the joiner's
To buy him a coffin,
But when she came back
The poor dog was laughing.

She took a clean dish
To get him some tripe,
But when she came back
He was smoking a pipe.

She went to the fishmonger's
To buy him some fish,
And when she came back
He was licking the dish.

She went to the ale-house
To get him some beer,
But when she came back
The dog sat in a chair.

She went to the tavern
For white wine and red,
But when she came back
The dog stood on his head.

She went to the hatter's
To buy him a hat,
But when she came back
He was feeding the cat.

She went to the barber's
To buy him a wig,
But when she came back
He was dancing a jig.

She went to the fruiterer's
    To buy him some fruit,
But when she came back
    He was playing the flute.

She went to the tailor's
    To buy him a coat,
But when she came back
    He was riding a goat.

She went to the cobbler's
    To buy him some shoes,
But when she came back
    He was reading the news.

She went to the seamstress
    To buy him some linen,
But when she came back
    The dog was spinning.

She went to the hosier's
    To buy him some hose,
But when she came back
    He was dressed in his clothes.

The dame made a curtsy,
    The dog made a bow;
The dame said, 'Your servant',
    The dog said, 'Bow-wow'.

Four-and-twenty tailors

Four-and-twenty tailors
Went to catch a snail,
The best man amongst them
Durst not touch her tail;
She put out her horns
Like a little kyloe cow,
Run, tailors, run! or she'll have you all
    e'en now!

Once I saw a little bird

Once I saw a little bird
Come hop, hop, hop!
So I cried: 'Little bird,
Will you stop, stop, stop?'

And was going to the window
To say, 'How do you do?'
But he shook his little tail
And away he flew.

I had a little dog

I had a little dog,
And they called him Buff!
I sent him to the shop
For a ha'p'orth of snuff;
But he lost the bag,
And spill'd the snuff,
So take that cuff!
And that's enough.

Gravy and potatoes

Gravy and potatoes
    In a good brown pot—
Put them in the oven,
    and serve them very hot!

17

Pea-straw and parsnips! Pussy's in the well!
The doggie's gone to Guildford—gone to buy a bell;
Dingle dingle dousy!
   Ding dong bell!
Laugh little mousey!
   Pussy's in the well!

Who put her in?
   Little Tommy Thin!
Who pulled her out?
   Little Tommy Stout!
What a naughty boy was that,
For to drown our pussy cat;
Who never did him any harm,
And caught all the mice
   in Grand-da's big barn.

Jack Sprat had a cat

Jack Sprat
   Had a cat,
It had but one ear;
   It went to buy butter,
When butter was dear.

This pig went to market

This pig went to market;
   This pig stayed at home;
This pig had a bit of meat;
   And this pig had none;
This little pig cried
   'Wee! wee! wee!
I can't find my way home.'

Pussy-cat Mole

Pussy-cat Mole
Jump'd over a coal,
And in her best petticoat
Burnt a great hole.
Poor Pussy's weeping,
She'll have no more milk,
Till her best petticoat's
Mended with silk!

Pretty Lambkin

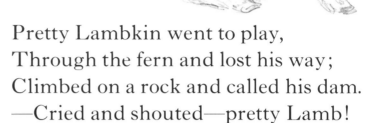

Pretty Lambkin went to play,
Through the fern and lost his way;
Climbed on a rock and called his dam.
—Cried and shouted—pretty Lamb!

Billy brown shrew

Billy brown shrew with the velvet clothes,
No eyes whatever and very long nose,
Call up your children as fast as you can!
—He whistled and twistled, that little brown man!

Oh who will come open this great heavy gate

'Oh who will come open this great heavy gate?
The hill fox yaps loud, and the moon rises late;
There's snow on the fell, and the flock's at the farm!'
'Little black Hoggie, we'll keep thee from harm!'

I had a little nut-tree

I had a little nut-tree,
Nothing would it bear
But a golden nutmeg,
And a silver pear.

The King of Spain's daughter
Came to visit me,
And all for the sake of
My little nut-tree!

I skipp'd over water,
    I danced over sea,
And all the birds in the
    air couldn't catch me.

Sieve my lady's oatmeal

Sieve my lady's oatmeal,
Grind my lady's flour,
Put it in a chestnut,
Let it stand an hour—
One may rush, two may rush,
Come, my girls, walk under the bush.

Little Poll Parrot

Little Poll Parrot
Sat in a garret
Eating toast and tea!
A little brown mouse
Jumped into his house,
And stole it all away!

The man in the wilderness

The man in the wilderness said to me,
'How many strawberries grow in the sea?'
I answered him as I thought good—
'As many red herrings as grow in the
    wood.'

Buz, quoth the blue fly

Buz, quoth the blue fly; hum, quoth
    the bee;
Buz and hum they cry, and so do we!

In his ear, in his nose,
    Thus do you see,
He ate the dormouse,
    Else it was thee.

We have a little garden

We have a little garden,
    A garden of our own,
And every day we water there
    The seeds that we have sown.

We love our little garden,
    And tend it with such care,
You will not find a faded leaf
    Or blighted blossom there.

Old Mr. Pricklepin

Old Mr. Pricklepin
    has never a cushion to
    stick his pins in,
His nose is black and his
    beard is gray,
And he lives in an ash stump
    over the way.

The Owl and the Pussy-cat

The Owl and the Pussy-cat went to sea
   In a beautiful pea-green boat,
They took some honey, and plenty of money,
   Wrapped in a five-pound note.
The Owl looked up to the stars above,
   And sang to a small guitar,
'O lovely Pussy! O Pussy, my love,
   What a beautiful Pussy you are,
       You are,
       You are!
   What a beautiful Pussy you are!'

Pussy said to the Owl, 'You elegant fowl!
   How charmingly sweet you sing!
O let us be married! too long we have tarried:
   But what shall we do for a ring?'

They sailed away for a year and a day,
   To the land where the Bong-tree grows,
And there in a wood a Piggy-wig stood,
   With a ring at the end of his nose,
       His nose,
       His nose,
   With a ring at the end of his nose.

'Dear Pig, are you willing to sell for one shilling
  Your ring?' Said the Piggy, 'I will.'
So they took it away, and were married next day
  By the Turkey who lives on the hill.
They dined on mince, and slices of quince,
  Which they ate with a runcible spoon;
And hand in hand, on the edge of the sand,
  They danced by the light of the moon,
        The moon,
        The moon,
  They danced by the light of the moon.

Hitty Pitty

Hitty Pitty within the wall,
Hitty Pitty without the wall;
If you touch Hitty Pitty,
Hitty Pitty will bite you!

Answer: *A nettle*

Arthur O'Bower

Arthur O'Bower has broken his band,
He comes roaring up the land!
The King of Scots with all his power,
Cannot turn Arthur of the Bower!

Answer: *The wind*

Hickamore, Hackamore

Hickamore, Hackamore, on the King's
    kitchen door;
All the King's horses, and all the
    King's men,
Couldn't drive Hickamore, Hackamore,
Off the King's kitchen door.

Answer: *A sunbeam*

Humpty Dumpty lies in a beck

Humpty Dumpty lies in the beck,
With a white counterpane round his neck,
Forty doctors and forty wrights,
Cannot put Humpty Dumpty to rights!

Answer: *An egg*

A house full, a hole full

A house full, a hole full!
And you cannot gather a bowl-full!

Answer: *Smoke*

Ninny Nanny Netticoat

Ninny Nanny Netticoat,
In a white petticoat,
 With a red nose—
The longer she stands,
 The shorter she grows.

Answer: *A candle*

As I went over Tipple-tine

Hum-a-bum! buzz! buzz! Hum-a-bum
   buzz!
   As I went over Tipple-tine
   I met a flock of bonny swine;

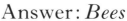

   Some yellow-nacked, some yellow backed!
   They were the very bonniest swine
   That e'er went over Tipple-tine.

Answer: *Bees*

Flour of England, fruit of Spain

   Flour of England, fruit of Spain,
   Met together in a shower of rain;
   Put in a bag tied round with a string,
If you'll tell me this riddle, I'll give you
   ring!

Answer: *A plum pudding*

Riddle me, riddle me, rot-tot-tote

Riddle me, riddle me, rot-tot-tote!
A little wee man, in a red red coat!
A staff in his hand, and a stone in his throat;
If you'll tell me this riddle, I'll give you a groat.

Answer: *A red cherry*

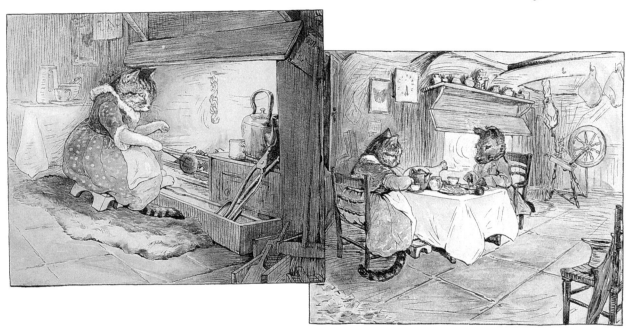

Pussy-cat sits by the fire

Pussy-cat sits by the fire;
    How should she be fair?
In walks the little dog,
    Says 'Pussy! are you there?

'How do you do, Mistress Pussy?
    Mistress Pussy, how do you do?'
'I thank you kindly, little dog,
    I fare as well as you!'

29

Big Box, little Box, Band- Box, Bundle

Big Box, little Box,
    Band-Box, Bundle!
You hold tight,
    and don't you tumble
When the train comes in,
    with a rush and a rumble.

The train came in,
    the barrow gave a trundle—
Off jumped Band-Box,
    little Box, Bundle!

The monster

There once was a
    large spotted weevil,
Whose looks were
    peculiarly evil.
But his looks were to blame—
He was perfectly tame,
Herbiverous,
    harmless and civil!

Diggory Diggory Delvet

Diggory Diggory Delvet!
A little old man in black
    velvet;
He digs and he delves—
You can see for yourselves
The mounds dug by Diggory
    Delvet.

Galeny, galeny, galene

Galeny, galeny, galene!
—Now what *is* that waving between
The nettles and docks on the green?

Potracket, potrack, potrack!
  The thing wavered forward and back—
Potrack! potrack! potrack!

Then the cowman crossed over the green,
And explained to Galeny, galene!

Old Mother Goose and her flat-footed daughter

Old Mother Goose and her flat-footed daughter
Live on the hill, near a fine spring of water;
Their grey-slated cottage is seen from the road,
Bench, tubs, doorway, chimney—a cheerful abode!

The peat smoke puffs up from their fire as we pass;
See, the blankets and sheets spread to bleach on the grass—
And when the sun shines, and the west wind blows high,
They'll wring out their washing, and hang it to dry.

The mushrooms

Nid, nid, noddy,
    we stand in a ring,
All day long,
    and never do a thing!
But nid nid noddy!
    we wake up at night,
We hop and we dance,
    in the merry moon-light!

Kadiddle, kadiddle, kadiddle

Kadiddle,
    kadiddle, kadiddle!
Come dance to my
    dear little fiddle?
(Kadiddle,
    kadiddle, kadiddle,
Come dancing along
    down the middle . . .
Oh silly Kadiddle,
    Kadiddle!)

There once was an amiable guinea-pig

There once was an amiable
   guinea-pig,
Who brushed back his hair like
   a periwig—

He wore a sweet tie,
   As blue as the sky—

And his whiskers and
   buttons
Were very big.

Little Jack Horner

Little Jack Horner
Sat in the corner
Eating a Christmas pie;
He put in his thumb,
And pulled out a plum,
And said, What a good boy am I!

Pig Robinson Crusoe

Poor Pig Robinson Crusoe!
Oh, how in the world could they do so?
They have set him afloat,
In a horrible boat,
Oh, poor Pig Robinson Crusoe!

Pussy Butcher

I'm a little 'Pussy Butcher' with a natty little cart,
My manners are superior, and my apron's clean and smart,
My billy-goat can trot a race with any tradesman's van—
—Then kindly do not call me common 'Cat's-meat Man'!

Babbity Bouster Bumble Bee

Babbity Bouster Bumble Bee!
   Fill up your honey bags, bring them to me!
Humming and sighing—with lazy wing
   Where are you flying—what song do you sing?

'Who'll buy my honey-pots? Buy them? Who'll buy?'
   Sweet heather honey—come weigh them and try!
—Honey-bag, honey-pot, home came she!
   Nobody buys from a big Bumble Bee!

There was an old snail with a nest

There was an old snail with a nest—
   Who very great terror expressed,
Lest the wood-lice all round
   In the cracks under-ground
Should eat up her eggs in that nest!

Her days and her nights were oppressed,
   —But soon all her fears were at rest;
For eleven young snails
   With extremely short tails,
Hatched out of the eggs in that nest.

Mrs. Tiggy-Winkle's ironing song

Lily-white and clean, oh!
With little frills between, oh!
   Smooth and hot—red rusty spot
Never here be seen, oh!

When the dew falls silently

When the dew falls silently
   And stars begin to twinkle,
Underneath the hollow tree
   Peeps poor Tiggy-Winkle.

Where the whispering waters pass—
   Her little cans twinkle,
Up and down the dewy grass
   Trots poor Tiggy-Winkle.

Three blind mice

Three blind mice, three
 blind mice,
 See how they run!
They all run after the farmer's
 wife,
And she cut off their tails with
 a carving knife,
Did ever you see such a thing
 in your life
 As three blind mice!

Fishes come bite!

Fishes come bite!
Fishes come bite!
I have fished all day;
I will fish all night.
I sit in the rain on my lily-leaf boat,
But never a minnow will bob my float.
Fishes come bite!

Appley Dapply

Appley Dapply, a little
brown mouse,
Goes to the cupboard in somebody's house.

In somebody's cupboard
There's everything nice,
Cake, cheese, jam, biscuits,
—All charming for mice!

Appley Dapply has little
sharp eyes,
And Appley Dapply is *so* fond
of pies!

Tabitha Twitchit is grown so fine

Tabitha Twitchit
  is grown so fine
She lies in bed
  until half past nine.
She breakfasts on muffins,
  and eggs and ham,
And dines on red-herrings
  and rasp-berry jam!!

Hey diddle dinketty

Hey diddle dinketty, poppetty, pet!
The merchants of London they wear scarlet;
Silk in the collar, and gold in the hem,
So merrily march the merchantmen!

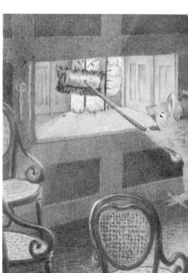

Three little mice sat down to spin

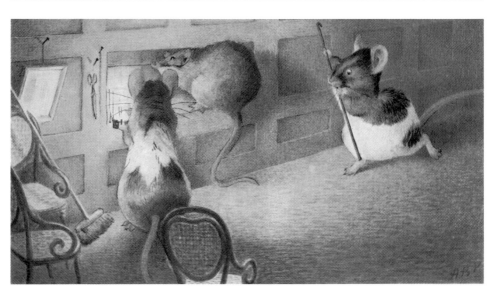

Three little mice sat down to spin,
Pussy passed by and she peeped in.
'What are you at, my fine little men?'
'Making coats for gentlemen.'
'Shall I come in and cut off your
    threads?'
'Oh, no! Miss Pussy, you'd bite off
    our heads!'

Dame get up and bake your pies

Dame get up and bake your pies,
    Bake your pies! bake your pies!
Dame get up and bake your pies,
    On Christmas Day in the morning.

Dame what makes your maidens lie?
    Maidens lie, maidens lie,
Dame what makes your maidens lie?
    On Christmas Day in the morning.

Dame what makes your ducks to die?
    Ducks to die, ducks to die,
Dame what makes your ducks to die?
    On Christmas Day in the morning.

Their wings are cut, and they cannot fly,
    Cannot fly, cannot fly,
Their wings are cut and they cannot fly,
    On Christmas Day in the morning.

Rushes grow green

Rushes grow green! rushes burn red!
We'll sup on rush candle, the little mice said.

42

To Market! To Market!

To Market! To Market!
  Now isn't this funny?
You've got a basket,
  and I've got some money!
—We went to market
  and I spent my money,
Home again! home again!
  Little Miss Bunny!

Hey diddle diddle

Hey diddle diddle,
The cat and the fiddle,
The cow jumped
  over the moon;
The little dog laughed
To see such sport,
And the dish ran away
  with the spoon.

The little black rabbit

Now who is this knocking
   at Cottontail's door?
Tap tappit! Tap tappit!
   She's heard it before?

And when she peeps out
   there is nobody there,
But a present of carrots
   put down on the stair.

Hark! I hear it again!
   Tap, tap, tappit! Tap
     tappit!
Why—I really believe it's a
   little black rabbit!

The horseshoe song

Tap, tap, tappitty! trot, trot, trod!
Sing Dolly's little shoes, on the hard high road!
Sing Quaker Daisey's sober pace,
Sing high-stepping Peter, for stately grace.
Phoebe and Blossom, sing softly and low,
   dear dead horses of long ago;
Jerry and Snowdrop;
   black Jet and brown
Tom and Cassandra,
   the pride of the town;
Bobby and Billy gray,
   Gypsy and Nell;
More bonny ponies
   than I can tell;
Prince and Lady,
   Mabel and Pet;
Rare old Diamond,
   and Lofty and Bet.
Dick, Duke, Sally,
   and Captain true,
Wisest of horses that
   ever wore shoe,
Shaking the road from the ditch to the crown,
When the thundering, lumbering larch comes down.

John Peel

D'ye ken John Peel with his coat so grey?
D'ye ken John Peel at the break of day?
D'ye ken John Peel when he's far, far away,
With his hounds and his horn in the morning.

'Twas the sound of his horn call'd me from my bed.
And the cry of his hounds has me oft times led;
For Peel's view halloa would 'waken the dead,
Or a fox from his lair in the morning.

John Smith, fellow fine

'John Smith, fellow fine!
Can you shoe this horse of mine?'
'Yes, Sir, that I can,
As well as any man!
Here a nail and here a prod,
Now the horse is well shod!'

I went into my grandmother's garden

I went into my
 grandmother's garden,
And there I found
 a farthing.
I went into my
 next door neighbour's,
There I bought a
 pipkin and a popkin,
A slipkin and a slopkin,
A nailboard, a sailboard,
And all for a farthing.

Tommy Tittle-mouse

I've heard that Tommy Tittle-mouse
 Lived in a tiny little house,
Thatched with a roof of rushes brown
 And lined with hay and thistle-down.

Walled with woven grass and moss,
 Pegged down with willow twigs across.
Now wasn't that a charming house
 For little Tommy Tittle-mouse?

47

The House that Jack built

This is the House that
Jack built.

This is the Malt
That lay in the House that
Jack built.

This is the Rat
That ate the Malt
That lay in the House that
Jack built.

This is the Cat
That killed the Rat
That ate the Malt
That lay in the House that
Jack built.

This is the Dog
That worried the Cat
That killed the Rat
That ate the Malt
That lay in the House that
Jack built.

This is the Cow
with the crumpled horn
That tossed the Dog
That worried the Cat
That killed the Rat
That ate the Malt
That lay in the House that
Jack built.

This is the Maiden all forlorn
That milked the Cow
with the crumpled horn
That tossed the Dog
That worried the Cat
That killed the Rat
That ate the Malt
That lay in the House that
Jack built.

This is the Man
    all tattered and torn
That kissed the Maiden
    all forlorn
That milked the Cow
    with the crumpled horn
That tossed the Dog
That worried the Cat
That killed the Rat
That ate the Malt
That lay in the House that
    Jack built.

This is the Priest
    all shaven and shorn
That married the Man
    all tattered and torn
That kissed the Maiden
    all forlorn
That milked the Cow
    with the crumpled horn
That tossed the Dog
That worried the Cat
That killed the Rat
That ate the Malt
That lay in the House that
    Jack built.

This is the Cock
    that crowed in the morn
That waked the Priest
    all shaven and shorn
That married the Man
    all tattered and torn
That kissed the Maiden
    all forlorn
That milked the Cow
    with the crumpled horn
That tossed the Dog
That worried the Cat
That killed the Rat
That ate the Malt
That lay in the House that
    Jack built.

Oh, what shall we have for supper, Mrs. Bond

'Oh, what shall we have for supper, Mrs. Bond?'
'There's geese in the larder, and ducks in the pond;
Dilly, dilly, dilly, dilly, come to be killed,
For you must be stuffed and my customers filled!'

'Send us the geese first, good Mrs. Bond,
And get us some ducks dressed out of the pond,
Cry, Dilly, dilly, dilly, dilly, come to be killed,
For you must be stuffed and my customers filled!'

'John Ostler, go fetch me a duckling or two,'
'Ma'am', says John Ostler, 'I'll try what I can do.'
'Cry, Dilly, dilly, dilly, dilly, come to be killed,
For you must be stuffed and my customers filled!'

'I have been to the ducks that swim in the pond,
But I found they won't come to be killed, Mrs. Bond;
I cried, Dilly, dilly, dilly, dilly, come to be killed,
For you must be stuffed and my customers filled!'

Mrs. Bond she flew down to the pond in a rage,
With plenty of onions and plenty of sage;
She cried, 'Dilly, dilly, dilly, dilly, come to be killed,
For you must be stuffed and my customers filled!'

She cried, 'Little wag-tails, come and be killed,
For you must be stuffed and my customers filled!
Dilly, dilly, dilly, dilly, come to be killed,
For you must be stuffed and my customers filled!'

The kettle's song

With pomp power and glory
  the world beckons vainly,
In chase of such vanities
  why should I roam?
While peace and content bless
  my little thatched cottage,
And warm my own hearth
  with the treasures of home.

Old King Cole

Old King Cole was a merry old soul,
And a merry old soul was he,
He called for his pipe
  And he called for his bowl,
And he called for his fiddlers three—

Fiddle fiddle fiddle!
  Went the fiddlers three,
Fiddle, fiddle, fiddle, fiddle, fee!
Oh there's none so rare
  As can compare
With King Cole and his fiddlers three!

Little lad, little lad

Little lad, little lad,
  where was't thou born?
Far off in Lancashire
  under a thorn,
Where they sup sour milk,
  in a ram's horn!

Shepherdess of fields on high

Shepherdess of fields on high,
    Drive in your thousand sheep!
Flocks that stray across the sky,
    And clouds that sail the deep!

The shepherd boy's song

Spring comes to the uplands, the cuckoo is calling,
Sweet gale and green withy unfolding their leaves.
There's honey bees humming and swallows a-coming
—Come back pretty wanderers! come nest 'neath the eaves!

Now Summer is smiling mid roses beguiling.
With hay cocks and harvest and 'taties to store,
Brave autumn comes prancing with fiddles and dancing
And leads the kern supper with jigs on the floor.

Blow cold winds of winter, we'll shutter the window!
Shine keen frosty starlight when tempests are stilled;
Is there snow on the door stane? Heap peats on the hearth stone!
Sing little black kettle—the year is fulfilled.

My father left me three acres of land

My father left me three acres of land,
  Sing ivy, sing ivy!
My father left me three acres of land,
  Sing holly go whistle and ivy!

I ploughed it with a ram's horn,
  Sing ivy, sing ivy!
I sowed it all over with one peppercorn,
  Sing holly go whistle and ivy!

I harrowed it with a bramble bush,
  Sing ivy, sing ivy!
And reaped it with my little penknife,
  Sing holly go whistle and ivy!

I got the mice to carry it to the mill,
  Sing ivy, sing ivy!
And thrashed it with a goose's quill,
  Sing holly go whistle and ivy!

My little old man and I fell out

My little old man and I fell out,
How shall we bring this matter about?
Bring it about as well as you can,
And get you gone, you little old man!

53

The Tom-tit's song

I made my nest in a hollow pear-tree,
Nobody lived there but Titmouse and me!

I lined that nest with feathers black and grey,
—There came a wicked sparrow and stole them half away!

Ten very tiny eggs, speckled white and red!
  Soft fluffy feathers hid them over-head.

Ten speckled white eggs and three speckled grey,
  Quite of different sizes in that nest soon lay.

I'm not good at counting—ten and one two three!
  It was very puzzling to Titmouse and me!

Thirteen little naked birds with yellow mouths gaped wide,
—And three of them *such* big ones—we looked at them with pride.

Calling for their breakfast—ten and one two three!
  Hard work providing for Titmouse and me—

But when their feathers came—what a shocking sight!
  Three of them were brown birds, mine are blue and white;

Three horrid sparrows, as greedy as could be!
  Crowding and imposing on Titmouse and me!

Greedier and noisier they grew every day—
  Just when we were desperate, the monsters flew away!

—Ten little tom tits, as merry as can be!
  Chasing one another round a Perry pear-tree!

Wassal, wassal, to our town

Wassal, wassal, to our town!
The cup is white and the ale is brown;
The cup is made of the ashen tree,
And so is the ale of the good barley.

Little maid, little maid, turn the pin,
Open the door and let us come in!

Blessed be the master of this house, and the mistress also,
And all the little babies that round the table grow!
Their pockets full of money, the cellars full of beer,
A merry Christmas to you, and a happy New Year!

Ladybird, ladybird, fly away home

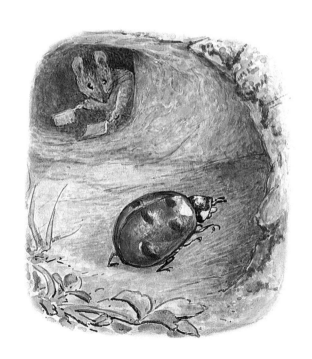

Ladybird, ladybird,
    Fly away home,
Your house is on fire
    And your children all gone;
All except one
    And her name is Ann,
And she has crept under
    The pudding pan.

Intery, mintery, cuttery, corn

Intery, mintery, cuttery, corn,
Apple seed and apple thorn;
Wine, brier, limber-lock,
Five geese in a flock,
Sit and sing by a spring,
O-U-T, and in again.

Spring

There came a lady
    from Fairy-land,
  Who carried a primrose
    in her hand;
The green grass leapt after,
    wherever she trod,
  And daisies and butter-cups
    danced on the sod.

Her locks were pale may-flowers,
    a sunbeam her nose;
  Her breath was the cowslip's, she'd bells on her toes;
Her eyes were blue violets, her lips were red flame,
  Her voice was the throstle's—and Spring was her name!

Hark! hark! the dogs do bark

Hark! hark!
The dogs do bark,
The beggars are come to town,
Some in tags
And some in rags
And one in a velvet gown!

Buttercup land

When swift cloud shadows race over the hills—
Where tinkling water leaps down the steep ghylls
On wide brown sands at the edge of the sea—
Little odd people come whisper to me!

Under the bracken and wood moss they peep,
And play in the moonlight when other folks sleep,
They hide in the sweet-smelling hay in the barn,
And under the wainscots and tubs at the farm.

Land of kind dreams,
    where the mountains are blue,
Where brownies are friendly
    and wishing comes true!
Through your green meadows
    they dance hand in hand—
—Little odd people
    of Buttercup Land.

As I walked by myself

As I walked by myself
And talked to myself,
Myself said unto me,
Look to thyself,
Take care of thyself,
For nobody cares for thee.

I answered myself,
And said to myself
In the self-same repartee,
Look to thyself,
Or not to thyself,
The self-same thing will be.

Publisher's note

Beatrix Potter's fondness for nursery rhymes revealed itself very early in her writing career. In 1901, before her successful *The Tale of Peter Rabbit* had been published by Frederick Warne & Co., she had written a second story for her ex-governess's little daughter, Freda Moore, which was so 'cram full' of nursery rhymes that she very wisely decided to have *The Tailor of Gloucester* privately printed the following year before submitting it to her publishers. As she suspected, they asked for cuts, and many of the rhymes were sacrificed. Because of this *The Tale of Squirrel Nutkin* became the second book in the series, but even here Beatrix Potter had managed to weave her favourite riddles into the plot.

In 1905 she and her editor, Norman Warne, were collaborating on a collection of rhymes to be called *Appley Dapply's Nursery Rhymes*, but tragically Norman died before the book could be completed. Some of these rhymes were traditional, others had been adapted by Beatrix Potter, but many were her own compositions. A few were published in the 1917 edition of *Appley Dapply's Nursery Rhymes*. Later in 1922 came a sequel, *Cecily Parsley's Nursery Rhymes*. But there were so many delightful poems in the 1905 collection, which children were missing, that we decided to combine the whole of this collection, the *Cecily Parsley* rhymes and the riddles from *Squirrel Nutkin*, with most of the rhymes from the original manuscript of *The Tailor of Gloucester*, from *The Fairy Caravan*, and jingles from some of the other tales, to make a book of Beatrix Potter's favourite nursery rhymes. Often just a line or two from a rhyme appeared in her stories, but we have quoted the full version here from James Orchard Halliwell's *The Nursery Rhymes of England*.

Nursery Rhymes taken from Beatrix Potter's works (page numbers refer to pages in this book; * after a poem indicates that it also appeared in the 1903 Warne edition of *The Tailor of Gloucester*, and ** that the rhyme also appeared in the 1917 Warne edition of *Appley Dapply's Nursery Rhymes*) From the original manuscript of *The Tailor of Gloucester*: Ride a cock-horse page 12; Old Mother Hubbard 15; Four-and-twenty tailors* 16; Once I saw a little bird* 17; I had a little dog 17; Jack Sprat had a cat 18; Pussy-cat Mole* 20; I had a little nut tree* 21; Seive my lady's oatmeal* 21; Little Poll Parrot 22; Buz, quoth the blue fly* 22; Little Jack Horner 34; Hey diddle dinketty* 39; Three little mice sat down to spin* 40; Dame get up and bake your pies* 42; Hey diddle diddle* 43; John Smith, fellow fine 46; I went into my grandmother's garden* 47; Oh, what shall we have for supper, Mrs. Bond 50; Old King Cole 51; Wassal, wassal, to our town 55; Intery, mintery, cuttery, corn 56; Hark! Hark! the dogs do bark 57. From *The Tale of Squirrel Nutkin*: The man in the wilderness 22; Hitty Pitty 25; Arthur O'Bower 26; Hickamore, Hackamore 26; Humpty Dumpty lies in a beck 27; A house full, a hole full 27; As I went over Tipple-tine 28; Flour of England, Fruit of Spain 28; Riddle me, riddle me, rot-tot-tote 29. From the 1905 *Appley Dapply* collection: Knitting 9; The mouse's find 10; If acorn-cups were tea-cups 11; I saw a ship a-sailing 12; The old woman who lived in a shoe** 13; The see-saw 13; Gravy and potatoes** 17; Pea-straw and parsnips, Pussy's in the well! 18; Pretty Lambkin 20; Billy brown shrew 20; Oh who will come open this great heavy gate? 21; Old Mr. Pricklepin** 23; Big Box, little box, Band Box, Bundle 30; The monster 30; Diggory Diggory Delvet 30; Galeny, galeny, galene 31; Old Mother Goose and her flat-footed daughter 31; The mushrooms 32; Kadiddle, kadiddle, kadiddle 32; There once was an amiable guinea-pig** 33; Pussy Butcher 34; Babbity Bouster Bumble Bee 35; There was an old snail with a nest 35; When the dew falls silently 36; Fishes come bite! 37; Appley Dapply** 38; Tabitha Twitchit is grown so fine 39; Rushes grow green 42; To Market! To Market! 43;

The little black rabbit** 44; Tommy Tittle-mouse 47; Shepherdess of fields on high 52; The Tom-tit's song 54; Spring 56; Buttercup land 57. From *Cecily Parsley's Nursery Rhymes*: Bow, wow, wow, whose dog art thou? 9; Goosey Goosey Gander 10; Cecily Parsley 14; This pig went to market 19; We have a little garden 23; Ninny Nanny Netticoat 27; Pussy-cat sits by the fire 29; Three blind mice 37. From a booklet published in *The History of the Writings of Beatrix Potter*: The Owl and the Pussy-cat 24. From *The Tale of Little Pig Robinson*: Pig Robinson Crusoe 34. From *The Tale of Mrs. Tiggy-Winkle*: Mrs. Tiggy-Winkle's ironing song 36. From *The Fairy Caravan*: The horseshoe song 45; John Peel 46; The House that Jack built 48; Little lad, little lad 51; My father left me three acres of land 53; As I walked by myself 58. From *Wag-by-Wa'*, 1943 version published in *The History of the Writings of Beatrix Potter*: The kettle's song 51. From *Wag-by-Wall*, 1944 Horn Book version: The shepherd boy's song 52. From *The Tale of Timmy Tiptoes*: My little old man and I fell out 53. From *The Tale of Mrs. Tittlemouse*: Ladybird, ladybird, fly away home 55.

Picture sources (appropriate illustrations have been taken from Beatrix Potter's works; page numbers refer to this book) From *Cecily Parsley's Nursery Rhymes* pages 9 (above), 10 (below, left), 14, 19, 23 (above and centre), 27 (below), 29, 37 (above); *Appley Dapply's Nursery Rhymes* 9 (below), 13 (above), 17 (below, left), 21 (detail, below, left) 23 (below), 30 (below), 33, 38, 44; *Beatrix Potter's Birthday Book* 10 (above, left), 21 (above), 48 (above), 53 (above), 56 (above, right); *The Tale of Mrs. Tiggy-Winkle* 10 (above, right), 36 (centre, left is a detail), 56 (below, right); *A History of the Writings of Beatrix Potter* 11 (above), 12 (centre and below), 22 (above, left), 24, 25 (above), 30 (centre, left), 31 (above), 42 (detail from rejected picture for *The Tale of Peter Rabbit*, above), 51 (centre, left); The Linder Collection, Book Trust, London, 11 (below), 17 (centre), 47 (below), 51 (above), 55 (above); *The Art of Beatrix Potter* 13 (below), 17 (detail, left), 28 (below), 32, 34 (detail, above), 40–41, 47 (above), 50 (details); Warne's collection 12 (above), 31 (below, right), 57 (below); *The Fairy Caravan* 15, 17 (detail, centre, right), 18 (below), 20 (detail, above, left), 34 (below, left), 39 (above, right), 45, 46, 49 (detail), 54 (above), 57 (detail, above); *The Tailor of Gloucester* 16 (left), 39 (below, left); *The Tale of Mr. Jeremy Fisher* 16 (detail, left), 37 (below), 42 (below); *The Tale of Peter Rabbit* 17 (detail, above, right), 54 (detail, below); *The Story of Miss Moppet* 18 (above); The Leslie Linder Bequest, the Victoria and Albert Museum, London, 20 (above, right and below, right), 31 (centre, left), 43 (above), 52, 58; *The Tale of Samuel Whiskers* or *The Roly-Poly Pudding* 21 (endpaper detail, centre, right), 48 (endpaper details, centre and below); *The Tale of Pigling Bland* 21 (detail, below, left); *The Tale of Johnny Town-Mouse* 22 (above, right); *The Tale of Mrs. Tittlemouse* 22 (below, right), 28 (repeated endpaper detail, above), 35 (above is a detail), 53 (below); *The Tale of Squirrel Nutkin* 25 (below), 26, 27 (above); *The Tale of Little Pig Robinson* 27 (centre), 34 (below, right); *Beatrix Potter's Address Book* 30 (above); *The Tale of the Pie and the Patty-pan* 39 (centre, left); *The Journal of Beatrix Potter* 51 (detail, below, right); *The Tale of Timmy Tiptoes* 53 (below); *Peter Rabbit's Almanac for 1929* (republished under the title *Peter Rabbit's Diary*) 56 (above, left).

THE ORIGINAL
PETER RABBIT BOOKS

BY
BEATRIX POTTER